TRIAL AND ERRORS

A MODERN COMIC PLAY

MERSIHA

Copyright © Mersiha
All Rights Reserved.

ISBN 978-1-63957-957-0

This book has been published with all efforts taken to make the material error-free after the consent of the author. However, the author and the publisher do not assume and hereby disclaim any liability to any party for any loss, damage, or disruption caused by errors or omissions, whether such errors or omissions result from negligence, accident, or any other cause.

While every effort has been made to avoid any mistake or omission, this publication is being sold on the condition and understanding that neither the author nor the publishers or printers would be liable in any manner to any person by reason of any mistake or omission in this publication or for any action taken or omitted to be taken or advice rendered or accepted on the basis of this work. For any defect in printing or binding the publishers will be liable only to replace the defective copy by another copy of this work then available.

To My Mother, Family, Friends & Teachers

Contents

Foreword — *vii*

Prologue — *ix*

1. Characters Of The Play — 1
2. Scene 1 — 2
3. Scene 2 — 4
4. Scene 3 — 10
5. Scene 4 — 14
6. Scene 5 — 18
7. Scene 6 — 22
8. Scene 7 — 26
9. Scene 8 — 29
10. Scene 9 — 32
11. Scene 10 — 35
12. Scene 11 — 39
13. Scene 12 — 42
14. Scene 13 — 45
15. Scene 14 — 48

Foreword

This play has fourteen scenes written in a sequence. This play is written only to evoke laughter among the readers and spectators. Read, watch and enjoy the play without any serious intention.

"I regard the theatre as the greatest of all art forms, the most immediate way in which a human being can share with another the sense of what it is to be a human being." said Oscar Wilde.

- Mersiha
dhiyamersiha@gmail.com

Prologue

"Life's but a walking shadow, a poor player
That struts and frets his hour upon the stage,
And then is heard no more. It is a tale
Told by an idiot, full of sound and fury,
Signifying nothing."

1
Characters of the Play

WOODY, the Carpenter
SPIKES, the Carpenter
MR.RICH, the Wealthy Man
BUTLER, the Housekeeper
REV.BENEDICT, the Priest
DR.SAWBONES, the Doctor
SPADE, the Gravedigger
MARK, the Teacher
RAIDER, Cousin to the teacher
ROOKY, Apprentice to RAIDER
KITH
A BOY
GARDENER
THE MAN IN WHITE CLOTHES
NEIGHBOUR (VOICE)
and EXTRAS

2
Scene 1

An empty room except for a stool in a corner on it where an empty old Candelabrum. On the wall above hangs a rosary with a cross. Voices hear outside.

WOODY (VOICE) : In the name of God we can begin SPIKES...

SPIKES (VOICE) : But all we need is money to begin, WOODY.

Hear knocks on the door

WOODY (VOICE) : Is anyone here?

SPIKES (VOICE) : I think... no one.

Hear footsteps

NEIGHBOUR (VOICE) : Hello, who are you? What do you want?

WOODY (VOICE) : We are carpenters of the nearby village. The man of the house bought from us a stool seven days before but paid nothing so far...

NEIGHBOUR (VOICE) : He is not here. Only six days before he had started a pilgrimage to the holy places of the world.

WOODY (VOICE) : (*astonishingly*) What?

NEIGHBOUR (VOICE) : Yes, to the places where God made miracles.

SPIKES (VOICE) : What is there to wonder at God's miracles, for he is God?

NEIGHBOUR (VOICE) : What?

SPIKES (VOICE) : For men this is impossible, but everything is possible for God. Well, when will be he back?

NEIGHBOUR (VOICE) : Mm... I think... I don't know... May be after getting the vision?

SPIKES (VOICE) : Where, in the heaven..? Okay. Tell him, if you happen to meet him that it is more important to visit people in need than to visit places where God made wonders. Let's move.

ppp

3
Scene 2

Inside an old fashioned spacious bedroom, MR.RICH is walking slowly to and fro across. He is a sturdy man in his seventies, bald headed, clean shaven but with a big moustache. BUTLER, the servant enters. He is a man in his forties with a thin, crooked body and of short stature.

BUTLER: Sir, Father is waiting outside..!

MR.RICH: Fetch him in.

BUTLER goes out. MR.RICH sits in the chair. BUTLER comes back with the priest. He is a thin figure without a trace of hair on his face. His eyebrows are very thick and his ears have brush-like hair. He is partially deaf and hears hardly anything behind his back.

REV. BENEDICT: Praise the lord! Greetings, sir!

MR.RICH: *(with smile)* Come Father, my dear friend, sit.

REV. BENEDICT: Not bad, what about you, how's your health sir?

Sits opposite to MR.RICH

MR.RICH: *(to BUTLER)* Bring some tea for him. *(Looking at the priest.)* Hope with sugar.

REV. BENEDICT: Yes, without Sugar. I'm not diseased but it is better to hide in a gutter than to be stung by wasps. Am

I correct? *(Laughs.)*

Exit BUTLER

Why did you send for me sir, anything important?

MR.RICH: *(loudly)* Yes, something important! I am decided to offer you...

A flash in the face of the priest

What to say... My sins!

REV. BENEDICT: What do you mean by this, Sir?

MR.RICH: *(loudly)* Confession!

REV. BENEDICT: Confession! It becomes out of fashion now. People find it very difficult to distinguish sins from their day-to-day doings.

MR.RICH: *(loudly)* You somehow get relieved, then.

REV. BENEDICT: Of course! In those days, I was very much distressed, for no man is ready to regret anything aloud. I heard nothing but big sighs.

BUTLER comes back with a tray and places it before them. MR.RICH nods him to leave. He goes out.

MR.RICH: *(sipping)* Ooh! Be cautious sir. It's very hot.

Unaware of him, the priest gulps a mouthful. His eyes turn red and wet. Looking at MR.RICH,

REV. BENEDICT: It's very hot.

MR.RICH: *(loudly)* Well, I want to tell you something confidential.

The priest sits straight to show his attentiveness.

The whole wealth of mine is not supposedly mine as you all think. I've betrayed many and murdered some to achieve this state of being. The people I've killed come together and sit on my bosom while I sleep, without a day's absence. I never slept peacefully for many years. *(Pause.)* I feel the stain of blood in every morsel of my food. Even this cup of tea smells blood to me.

At once, the priest looks into the cup in his hand. Grimacing, he sets back it in the tray.

I don't want to deceive anyone, anymore. I want to get rid of this cursed wealthy life. Before that, I want to confess all my sins to someone like you. Hope you'll consider...

REV. BENEDICT: *(interrupting)* But sir..?

Enter BUTLER

BUTLER: Doctor's come sir, waiting outside.

MR.RICH: Send him in.

Exit BUTLER

REV. BENEDICT: What did he say?

MR.RICH: *(loudly)* The doctor has come, waiting outside.

REV. BENEDICT: *(frowning)* Oh! That fellow! Wretched being! I think I shouldn't be here. May I leave now sir? *(Stands up.)*

MR.RICH: No Sir. Sit.

MR.RICH gestures him to sit. DR.SAWBONES enters. He appears younger than the priest, handsome enough to be a physician.

DR.SAWBONES: *(looking at the priest)* Oh! You're here, the heaven's gatekeeper. Greetings, sir!

MR.RICH: Doctor, please don't...

REV. BENEDICT: God bless you, DR.SAWBONES.

DR.SAWBONES: Let it be, MR.BENEDICT.

The doctor goes to DR.RICH and inspects him with his stethoscope and speaks loudly

DR.SAWBONES: I think someone has troubled you so far...

MR.RICH: Why doctor?

DR.SAWBONES: The heart rate is too high. Be calm, sir. Take rest. Don't mingle with menaces.

At once, the priest places his hand on MR.RICH's forehead and starts to pray. DR.SAWBONES, with grim face, hands a tablet to MR.RICH.

DR.SAWBONES: Take this now, Sir. *(loudly)* Mere words do not alter anything.

REV. BENEDICT: *(vehemently)* My words are more powerful than your wrapped lime stones.

DR.SAWBONES: *(loudly)* Is it? Do you think so reverend friend? *(Laughs.)* No rational being can accept it sir. *(Laughs.)*

REV. BENEDICT: *(angrily)* What? You impure pup of a bitch!

DR.SAWBONES has startled by this unexpected reaction and words from the priest. MR.RICH is also surprised. The doctor's face turns red and is sweating all over. He shivers and sighs, looking furiously back at the priest.

REV. BENEDICT: *(calmly)* I beg your pardon my friend. Check your pulse and look at your face now. You can realise now the power of words, spoken. *(Pause.)* Thinking against the divine is not rational as you all abnormal people think. *(Looking upward at the ceiling.)* He, the one is beyond all our scarce senses.

The doctor prepares to leave.

DR.SAWBONES: Well, Sir, I'm leaving. *(Looking at the priest and to MR.RICH.)* Keep yourself out of reach of germs sir and don't speak unnecessarily.

MR.RICH: Sit down doctor. Calm yourself. *(Calls.)* BUTLER..!

DR.SAWBONES: Thank you, sir. But I need to go now.

Enter BUTLER

MR.RICH: *(to BUTLER)* Go with him.

The doctor hands his box to BUTLER and rushes out.

MR.RICH: *(loudly)* You were too harsh to him. I didn't expect that from you.

REV. BENEDICT: He speaks always against God as if an employed enemy to him.

MR.RICH: *(shaking his head, loudly)* No... No... He has his own freedom to get away from where we are all stapled.

REV. BENEDICT: But freedom should be restricted to some extent. Otherwise, it'll damage that of the other's.

BUTLER comes back, running, with a cry.

BUTLER: Doctor slipped into the ditch. He and his clothes are all stained.

REV. BENEDICT: *(grinning)* And where's he now?

BUTLER: He wants to go home. He doesn't want to wash him here.

MR.RICH: And why did you come back?

BUTLER: He doesn't want anyone to go with him.

MR.RICH: Okay, you go now.

Exit BUTLER

REV. BENEDICT: God often confirms his presence to his offenders. He is great. Praise the lord.

MR.RICH: *(loudly)* Okay, leave it. Come back to my remission.

REV. BENEDICT: Yes sir, I'm there. What am I supposed to do?

MR.RICH: *(loudly)* I need your help to help the helpless.

REV. BENEDICT: Sir, I'm always ready to part with the entire burden you have. Don't hesitate to put your responsibilities upon my shoulders. I'm ready to climb up a pine tree and jump down from there for you.

Silence. Both of them look straight into each other's eyes for some time.

MR.RICH: *(loudly)* I'm thinking of sharing my wealth to the welfare of the poor. I appoint you as the power of attorney to it. Do you agree?

REV. BENEDICT: *(happily)* Oh God! With great pleasure, sir! How much do you want to allocate sir?

MR.RICH: *(loudly)* I'm going to give one percent of my monthly income...

REV. BENEDICT: *(stands in despair but with smile)* Praise the lord. I'll do sir. I've to go now. We'll meet soon. God bless you.

He goes out hastily not waiting for any reply. MR.RICH starts to drink the remaining tea. Moments later, BUTLER comes in, as before, with a cry.

BUTLER: Father slipped into the ditch. He and his clothes are all stained.

MR.RICH: Where's he now?

BUTLER: He ran away, sir.

MR.RICH: What?

BUTLER: He stood up, looked around and left the place swiftly as if the cat out of mud. He thought that no one has noticed him but I did.

MR.RICH: God often confirms his presence to his admirers too. Well, you go now. Don't send anyone inside. I've to take rest, a long complete rest.

BUTLER goes out with the tray of empty cups in his hands. MR.RICH remains there where he is.

ppp

4
Scene 3

A small cabin. Wooden planks and boards are all over. WOODY, a man in his twenties is nailing a box. In the corner of the room, SPIKES, a man born a few years before WOODY, is painting a coffin.

WOODY: I saw her today in the church.

SPIKES: As usual!

WOODY: I spoke with her.

SPIKES: Unusual!

WOODY: She's allowed me to love her.

SPIKES: Ph! *(Nodding his head up and down.)* Women are always like this, travelling in a wagon which has both its ends, the fronts, can make their way opposite at any time.

WOODY: *(confused)* What are you saying..? I get nothing.

SPIKES: Leave it. What about her?

WOODY: She too loves me.

SPIKES: What for?

WOODY: For what..? Love flourishes not out of reasons.

SPIKES: Yes, I know. It has no reason at all but I find nothing worthy in you for getting loved.

WOODY: She wants to live like us, casually. She, fed-up with the way she lives systematically, wants to live with me anywhere under the sky.

SPIKES: Under the sky..! But it'll expose everything. Don't try that for our culture's sake.

WOODY looks at him severely and continues his work.

Some of the rich people prefer simple living just not to get bored with their wealth. Moreover, plateaus seem beautiful from the hills.

Silence for some time. SPIKES has finished his work and sat beside WOODY.

WOODY: You're a cynic. Aren't you? Speak always against everything. Try to love someone and it would reform you. *(Pause.)* Why don't you marry someone, if never want to love.

SPIKES: Being a bachelor, all through one's life, is a bit difficult but only a bit. It is sensible to shield our senses to safeguard ourselves from sufferings.

WOODY: You speak always nonsense.

SPIKES: Past nonsenses are present philosophies.

WOODY: There are people who could believe everything as maxims, if the words are spoken with some stubborn stress. Please stop your foolish philosophies always unrelated to the context.

SPIKES: Indeed, wise men appear as fools because they know everything but nothing in particular. It's better to be a fool rather than mad.

SPIKES starts to paint the box, WOODY has been mending. A dirty boy in torn clothes enters mechanically with a paper in his hand.

THE BOY: *(looking at WOODY)* Who's SPIKES here?

WOODY turns towards SPIKES who remains in his work without showing any interest in the happenings around him.

He has a message.

The boy has thrown the paper inside the box that SPIKES is painting. Both the boy and WOODY exchange smiles and with a wink, the boy rushes out. SPIKES notices the paper and continues to work. Silence for some time.

WOODY: You've to respond.

SPIKES: For what?

WOODY: You've received a message and your respect towards is not...

SPIKES: That messenger is not a prophet or anything of that sort. If you're curious to know the content of it, then read it for my sake.

At once, WOODY takes the paper and reads it aloud.

WOODY: *(reading)* Dear friend of my dearest, Greetings. Hope you well. Your friend is very much in need of you, for you're the only intelligent person around him and reputable too. You've to help him in building our palace of love. I think he is not potential enough to do things individually. Please consider this as a humble request from an honourable sister. Help him whenever he is hopeless. Your charming sister, Miss. Fancy. Note: If we get married, we would like to name our son as SPIKES with your permission.

He stops reading and looks at SPIKES who's wiping his hands with a piece of cloth.

SPIKES: How much did you pay him?

WOODY: To what?

SPIKES: You're supposed to ask 'to whom?'

WOODY: *(desperately)* Then, to whom?

SPIKES: To that dirty boy who's brought this yell for help from your belle.

WOODY: You're too suspicious that you suspect anything including your soul mate.

SPIKES: Only suspicions sustain truth alive.

WOODY: Okay! I admit. I myself wrote this letter but how did you find it out?

SPIKES: It's very simple. Before marriage, women never praise their chosen men's friends at any cost though they do it after. Moreover, she's been made my sister twice in that small piece of paper. Only, friends can make such things. They're very conscious to introduce ladies as sisters to their bosom pals.

WOODY: I request you to stop such too much of thinking.

SPIKES: But solutions are there in thinking. If it gets stopped, problems never exist to get solved. How can I help you then?

WOODY: *(happily)* Really, have you decided to help me in my love? Fantastic! You'll get into heavens by being a part of the divinity. Now on, please think something purposefully for me.

SPIKES: Well, but sometimes my stomach pulls back my mind to go forward. I've to feed me now.

WOODY: Come. Today is yours day. I'll feed you anything you want. Let's feast.

They exit.

ppp

5
Scene 4

Back of the church, in the corner of the graveyard is SPADE, the gravedigger's hut. WOODY and SPIKES are standing in front of the hut.

WOODY: There is no difference between the stray dogs and us.*(Silence.)* I think it's my baseless being, the iron curtain around me for her love to penetrate.

SPIKES: What base?

WOODY: Everything that is important for an ideal man, especially for an unmarried man. I don't even have a family at all.

SPIKES: The fact is... grown-up orphans are the most blessed beings on earth.

WOODY: And I've not properly been educated.

SPIKES: Nothing's lost. Arrogance and egoism are some of the side effects of the overdosed formal education. You could not have spoken like this to a fellow carpenter and accept you as 'nothing' if you were taught by a high school teacher. Moreover, classroom education would make our knowledge narrow.

Enter SPADE from the hut.

SPADE: What are you preaching, SPIKES?

SPIKES: Preaching! I'm just a practical man.

SPADE looks at WOODY who in turn expressed a serious smile.

SPADE: What makes him smile like a camel?

SPIKES: He's been deserted!

SPADE: Lovers always enjoy being distressed. They want to be with burdensome hearts but the real victims are the people around them, especially, their bosom pals.

WOODY: *(angrily)* Please, you just stop. Don't warm yourselves with someone's sighs.

SPIKES: *(to SPADE)* All he wants is to be richer than his beloved one. Do you have any strategies with you for that?

SPADE: *(staring at him severely)* If they get buried close by, I'll place an extra flower on his grave. That much is what I can do to make him richer than her.

SPIKES: I'm speaking with you seriously.

SPADE: It is possible but he's to wait till some wonders unearthed. I can help you but nowadays people don't let them get buried easily.

SPIKES: You could not help him even this whole village gets buried by you. She is not anyone but the daughter of our village don.

SPADE: *(with wide open eyes)* You're too ambitious WOODY. Oh! The man! His name itself is rich. You better forget her. *(Silence.)* Do you know my story, my own real untold life story?

Both WOODY and SPIKES nod their heads negatively.

(Looking at the sky.) Sit down.

They sit on a log of a tree nearby.

In my teenage days, I was homeless, work-less and worthless being more or less like a tramp. After some expeditions, I was employed to a cobbler. Most of the days, he had mended his own shoes and gave me wages nothing but only one seventh of his rationed food. His vendor wife used to beat me, pinch me and kick me whenever she did them all to her husband. She wanted me to leave him as she thought my presence there made him lazy. I too had the thought. Day-by-day, both his body and character started to turn into a sloth. *(Pause.)* Do you know what made me there to remain even after such a disgusting state of mine?

SPIKES: Their daughter!

SPADE: *(excited)* It's great SPIKE! How come you know?

SPIKES: What else there would be? I think you've forgotten the circumstance on where you started the story.

WOODY: You SPIKE! Don't interrupt. You continue, SPADE.

SPADE: She was very calm, quiet and pale, unlike her mother. She resembled exactly the oblique-headed women painted in the church portraits. We used to talk whenever her mother had not been found anywhere around in the village. Our love started to grow secretly like armpit hairs.

SPIKES: Disgusting!

SPADE: She was ready to come with me anywhere away from her mother's reach. *(Pause.)* At last, we eloped from there after lunch in one fine Wednesday. No one in the village thought that we were eloping. We pretended that we were actually playing. I ran behind her as if I was trying to catch her. We exchanged roles till some distance covered in our long journey. In that way, we reached a village far away from where we had begun...

Enter the gardener of MR.RICH's house hurriedly.

THE GARDENER: Oh! You people are here at last. I was searching for quarter of an hour. You've to go with a coffin to MR.RICH's house. He's dead.

WOODY: *(startled)* What?

THE GARDENER: *(looking at SPADE)* You dig a fine grave close to that of MRS.RICH.

The gardener goes out.

SPADE: *(frowning)* RICH is dead! Incredible! Only yesterday, I spoke with him. Pch! Unfortunate!

SPIKES: What is there to surprise at? If you happen to meet him tomorrow, then it'll be an unusual thing. Anyhow, some little sparks of fortune in your way, WOODY. Father of your fiancé is expired. Moreover, he's given us some work. Let's move.

WOODY: *(pretends to sob)* Great man! It's unfortunate to die at this age. I feel the hurt of her heart.

SPIKES: Don't act too much. I know you well. Some how the man provided us bread for somedays.

They Exit.

SPADE: *(looking at the sky)* Why do you call back the good ones so soon? Anyway, thanks a lot for making this day, fine. *(Pause.)* Someone has to die for someone other to live, invincible pattern.

ppp

6
Scene 5

A day later, in front of the church, the Priest and SPADE.

REV.BENEDICT: It's better to make our life, a glass built house than to a stone built. In the sense, we shouldn't be secret stuffed sacks. It'll make breathing difficult.

SPADE: But glass houses can be easily damaged.

Enter WOODY and SPIKES. Both greet the father together loudly.

Good morning, father!

REV.BENEDICT: God bless you sons.

WOODY: *(loudly)* Father, is there any problem in MR.RICH's house?

REV.BENEDICT: Yes, SPADE, a precious stone from MR.RICH's locker is lost after his funeral. It is worthier than that of the whole property of MR.RICH's family. The family members accuse each other and everyone unanimously made BUTLER as the scapegoat.

WOODY: *(loudly)* The housekeeper..?

REV.BENEDICT: Yes. I believe that it would be somewhere in the house itself. If anyone has stolen it, there's no way to make use of. He could be easily captured. Everyone searched in and out of the house inch by an inch.

SPIKES: *(grinning)* Did they look into the locker?

No one paid any attention to him.

WOODY: The thief can go abroad and prosper out of it, father!

REV.BENEDICT: But I don't find anyone who could do such things in our village.

Enter a boy shouting.

THE BOY: (*loudly*)Father! Father! The doctor asked you to go to his house immediately, now.

REV.BENEDICT: (*frowning*) Daughter! Whose daughter?

THE BOY: (*loudly again*) The doctor asked you to go to his house immediately, now.

REV.BENEDICT: Oh, Doctor! Is there anyone in his house?

THE BOY: (*loudly*)I don't know father. He told me nothing else. He asked you to...

REV.BENEDICT: Well! See you all. *(To the boy.)* Come along.

Exit the priest and the boy.

SPIKES: Is the doctor sick or anything?

SPADE: How do I know? May be he...

WOODY: Ok! Leave it SPADE. You do continue with your ever untold real story.

SPADE: Sit then.

All the three sit-down.

Where did I stop?

WOODY: You reached a village far away from where you began.

SPADE: *(recollecting)* Yes, I was there. I didn't know what to do further. My pockets were empty but for a fistful of soil from my homeland.

WOODY: Soil..?

SPADE: Yes, a symbolic symbol of my patriotism from my home-village.

WOODY: Really! You too have all such ideals?

SPADE: Why WOODY? What are you wondering at? An ideal citizen of a land which brought me to such level, I've to respect that, no? Patriotism made me mourn for a long time, then.

WOODY: *(looking at SPIKES)* Say something...

SPIKES: I don't find any reason behind the term patriotism. It's a cunning veil upon the foibles of a land. It urges the citizens to proud of everything, good or bad to him. It's just an imaginary instinct implied upon us.

WOODY: You continue SPADE. Did what further?

SPADE: We went to a farm in search of some job. The landlord was very much impressed upon us. He gave us work in the field and a small hut to live in.*(Silence.)*

WOODY: Does the fairy tale end here?

SPADE: No! (*Pause.*) One is not born but rather becomes a demon. Some days passed happily as you all web things in your mind. One day, the landlord gave me a basketful of brinjals and twenty three rupees to quit the place, ever leaving my lady for him there. I deliberately refused to do so for half an hour. She was innocent enough to believe his master's voice. She asked me to leave the place for the sake of our fortune. I was listening to her words as dumbly as a statue. Even before she was finishing her words, they unleashed their furious hounds to chase me out. I ran from there as fast as I can. *(Sobs and sighs.)*

Enter BUTLER

Oh! BUTLER! We've heard unusual things about you.

BUTLER: *(looking around)* What did you hear? Pch! My reputations were all lost.

SPADE: Did you steal anything from there?

BUTLER: *(astonishingly)* From where?

SPIKES: From there, where you lost all your reputations!

BUTLER: Do you all believe that ruthless scandal?

SPADE: Then, what do we do?

BUTLER: *(in whispering tone)* Do you know where those stones are now?

WOODY: Then you're the real raven!

BUTLER: Please folks, stop rowing from the shores itself. No one stole those things. They're in MR.RICH's stomach itself.

The three astonishingly look at him.

Yes, the stones are the cause for his death. He killed himself using that.

WOODY: Is it so? How was it possible?

BUTLER: I was there near his death bed. The doctor's report intended that the cause for death is vein burst. No one knows the reason for that vein burst but I.

ppp

7
Scene 6

In doctor's house, the doctor is sitting opposite to the priest and the village school teacher, MARK. In between them is a table.

REV.BENEDICT: But how did you come to the conclusion that he's dead because of that stones?

DR.SAWBONES: *(loudly)* I knew it on that day itself and the loss of the stones confirmed and stood beside my discovery. His people prevented me to do postmortem and buried him as quickly as they could. I was helpless in this regard.

REV.BENEDICT: Then what is the use of discussing it now?

DR.SAWBONES: *(whispering)* We can make use of the stones if you co-operate with us.

REV.BENEDICT: What?

DR.SAWBONES: *(murmuring to himself)* Oh, how can I tell a secret to these ears? *(Comes near to the priest.)* We can make use of the stones if you co-operate with us.

REV.BENEDICT: What do you mean by it?

MARK: *(looking around, loudly)* If we dig him out, then the stones are ours. What does he do with them anymore?

REV.BENEDICT: *(angrily)* What?

DR.SAWBONES: *(loudly)* We, all the three, can get something out of it.

The priest stands up preparing to leave.

REV.BENEDICT: Do you think all these vestments I wear are for fashion? Oh! What a crime do you want me to engage in?

MARK: *(loudly)* What crime is there to fear at? Is it a crime to swallow the edibles that fall into our mouth? Moreover, crime and all such things are manmade. Beheading people in a war-field is not a criminal act according to manmade laws, even the God-made.

REV.BENEDICT: It is a sin. I am not brought up to do such things.

MARK: *(loudly)* God doesn't want anyone good at all times. If so, He is supposed to create us perfect. He makes us to entertain himself at our follies. That's why we are here.

The priest looks at the doctor questioningly, turns to MARK and sits.

REV.BENEDICT: I am here to preach you only good...

DR.SAWBONES: *(loudly)* Only to preach..?

REV.BENEDICT: No, also to practice.

MARK: Good beings are those who've not yet got any chances to do sins whereas the bad beings have. That's the only difference.

REV.BENEDICT: I cannot accept whatever are the reasons for this to be done. I think you try to make me as a shield for your sins.

DR.SAWBONES: *(angrily)* You..!*(Making himself calm, loudly.)* Do you want those stones remain there in the graves forever uselessly to anyone?

REV.BENEDICT: Better, we can inform it to his family members.

MARK: *(whispering to the doctor)* Better, we can bury him alive.

DR.SAWBONES: *(loudly to the priest)* What rubbish are you talking sir? Do you want them to abduct our fortune?

REV.BENEDICT: Why? It is their own wealth and they have every right to abduct it.

DR.SAWBONES: *(loudly)* Who? Does your god give them the rights? Do they shed sweat for it? They are rich enough to remain idle for generations but we are not. We have to toil for generations to come. We have to grab opportunities. If we fail, nothing can give us hand to lift, for fortune knocks the door only once. Only the strongest could survive and now the richest.

The priest stands again and moves across the room. He drinks water and returns to the chair where he was seated.

REV.BENEDICT: *(scratching his forehead)* But..?

Both the doctor and the teacher wink and exchange smiles to each other.

MARK: *(loudly)* Don't worry father! We can visit Vatican and confess with the Pope himself for our sins, if we are rich enough to do. *(Silence.)*

REV.BENEDICT: Then, how will you unbury him?

DR.SAWBONES: *(loudly)* You don't worry all about that. There is a right man to do all such thing. Your part to play is to keep the graveyard closed for a whole night.

REV.BENEDICT: Closed..! Who is that person you've remarked now?

MARK: *(loudly)* My cousin! RAIDER is his name...

DR.SAWBONES: *(interrupting)* The most wanted in the town.

REV.BENEDICT: *(looking upward)* God, forgive me in advance. We do not know what we are doing.

DR.SAWBONES: *(loudly)* We are going to perform our plot at night, tomorrow. *(To the priest, loudly.)* Better you stop speaking to anyone, now on.

8
Scene 7

In the town, an employment office. A long queue in front of a counter that is showing a placard 'Application for Jobs'. Men of all types and ages are standing there. Some men, with either of their legs lifting, denote their standing hours together. A man in pure white clothes is wandering across the hall and in between the queue searching for something. A new man decently dressed adds himself in the queue.

THE NEW MAN: *(to the man just one before him, pointing to the man in white clothes)* What is that man doing here?

THE OTHER MAN: *(not looking back)* I don't know.

THE NEW MAN: *(to the man in white)* Hello, Excuse me, have you lost anything here?

THE SEARCHING MAN: Nothing!

THE NEW MAN: Then, why are you searching?

THE SEARCHING MAN: To find whether anything has been lost.

THE NEW MAN: Oh! I see! Crazy fellow! *(To the man before him)* By what name I can call you?

THE OTHER MAN: By the same name everyone calls me.

THE NEW MAN: *(sarcastically)* Well sir, please step down from my foot.

THE OTHER MAN: *(looking back)* Oh! Sorry, I'm extremely sorry. I thought that I have grown up an inch.

He turns and turns back again to shake his hand

THE NEW MAN: *(shaking hands)* I'm RAIDER:?

THE OTHER MAN: I'm KITH, fine.

Some people leisurely comes and forms a separate queue

RAIDER: Who are they?

KITH: They are people given reservation.

RAIDER: *(surprisingly)* What for..?

KITH: Their forefathers might be mouse hunters.

RAIDER: Do you not come under any such reservation categories?

KITH: No. My grandfathers never hunt anything, cursed beings, us!

RAIDER: The government is going to pass a bill very soon to give reservation for those who have been living in the upstairs of a two-storied building for six years.

KITH: But my house is in the ground floor.

RAIDER: Unfortunate! You have to wait till the time to come up. People who use only cow ghee to fry their food are also getting reservation now.

The reservation queue gradually decreases where the main queue remains idle.

(looking at his wrist) Oh! It's already 4.30 now. Just a half an hour remains for the counter to be closed. I think it's useless to remain here.

KITH: No, sir. Keep your hope alive. They will extend the time.

RAIDER: I'm leaving anyhow.

He prepares to leave. The man in front of KITH also leaves and following him, many other in front of him start leaving. Just the first three people of the queue remains along with KITH in the queue. The peon comes and places a board, 'CLOSED', behind KITH.

KITH: Oh my goodness, blessed I am.

He eagerly looks at the counter and his turn comes a few minutes later. He put his hand in the pant pocket to take his purse out, searches hastily all over his entire body only to find the purse missing, screaming.

Oh my purse! I've lost it. Excuse me sir.

But there is shutter in the counter which has been already closed.

THE MAN IN WHITE CLOTHES: Have you lost anything?

KITH desperately sinks in the nearby chair while the man in white clothes laughs out loudly. Meanwhile, a man with a piece of paper in his hand enters into the room, hurriedly. He is of a thin figure with crooked nose and flat chin.

RAIDER: Hey! ROOKY.

ROOKY: You have a message from your teacher cousin. He wants you to go there immediately now. He has an important work for you there.

RAIDER: *(surprisingly)* My teacher cousin..? (To himself) He has not called me over these years. (To ROOKY) Okay, come along.

They leave.

☙☙☙

9
Scene 8

Inside the church, REV.BENEDICT, with closed eyes, is praying alone. Enter SPADE.

SPADE: Father! Father! Do you hear me father? *(whispering)* What the man is alive or not? *(loudly)* Father! *(He touches him. There is no movement in his body)* Father! *(He starts to shake him up)*

REV.BENEDICT: *(waking)* Ooh!

SPADE: *(loudly)* Father, are you sleeping? Why did you send for me?

REV.BENEDICT: Yes, you have a work to do. Tomorrow you go to the church in the town. Stay there for a night and come back, the day after *(Pause.)* or whenever you want. Take this letter with you. You will be permitted.

SPADE: *(loudly)* Why father? What for?

REV.BENEDICT: Don't ask me questions. Do what I say! Keep this with you. *(He gives some coins to him)*

SPADE: *(hesitates)* Father, but..?

REV.BENEDICT: What..? Go!

SPADE resists going.

SPADE: *(loudly)* But I have an important work here, father.

REV.BENEDICT: *(angrily)* What important work is there for you here? Are you going to resurrect anyone?

SPADE: *(loudly, but in in a whispering tone)* I have something to say you, father.

REV.BENEDICT: What?

SPADE: *(comes very close to REV.BENEDICT:)* Please father, come out of the church. It should not be revealed here.

REV.BENEDICT: It is about what?

SPADE: It is about MR.RICH's death.

REV.BENEDICT: *(furiously)* What..?

SPADE: Yes father, about MR.RICH's death. He died not because of burst of blood vessels alone. There was a cause. He swallowed some poisonous stones, precious too.

REV.BENEDICT: *(absent mindedly)* I know all about that.

SPADE: How do you father? Did BUTLER tell you anything about..?

REV.BENEDICT: No... Yes...

He scratches his forehead. Both of them remain silent, looking deeply into each other's eyes.

SPADE: Is there any sort of sin in making use of some found treasure, father?

REV.BENEDICT: *(staring at him)* Make sure to whom you are speaking with. Go away? *(SPADE slowly starts to move)* Come back..! You do one thing. You take out the body tomorrow. DR.SAWBONES wants to find the reason for his death. But it should be confidential. No one should know except us.

SPADE: Who are all that us father?

REV.BENEDICT: We three and MARK.

SPADE: What is the need for a teacher in this matter, father?

REV.BENEDICT: Please don't ask me anything. Where is that BUTLER now?

SPADE: He is with the coffin makers.

REV.BENEDICT: What?

SPADE: With SPIKES and WOODY!

REV.BENEDICT: Do they know anything about this..?

SPADE: *(loudly)* Yes father, they do.

REV.BENEDICT: *(angrily)* Pch..! Does the whole village know about it? Anyone else..?

SPADE: *(loudly)* No father, no one else.

REV.BENEDICT: You go now. Don't discuss anything about this anymore to anyone. *(SPADE turns to move)* Wait..! Don't tell them about your tomorrow's task.

SPADE: Okay, father.

REV.BENEDICT: Give those coins I've given you.

SPADE returns the coins to him and goes out. REV.BENEDICT waits calmly until SPADE goes out and rushes out through the opposite door.

ppp

10
Scene 9

Same as in the third scene. SPIKES and WOODY are working in their room. BUTLER is sitting in the middle of the room on an upside down box.

WOODY: Why don't we dig that grave today itself?

BUTLER: No, no, the plot should not be altered at any rate. Then, things would all get ruined.

WOODY: I'm saying this because...

SPIKES: Because?

WOODY: The body would decompose. May be the worms and germs will eat the stones too.

BUTLER: *(laughing)* Ha... ha... ha... how innocent you are WOODY? The worms never come near those stones. They know, they would also die like the corpse, if they eat them.

SPIKES: I know the true reason for his haste.

BUTLER: What is it?

SPIKES: He is very much in need of money to marry.

BUTLER: But it needs a girl to marry, no?

SPIKES: Yes indeed. But do you prefer him as your son-in-law if you are a wealthy business dog, having a teenage daughter?

BUTLER: Why not? I certainly would if I'm.

SPIKES: Oh! Everyone is a socialist and support socialism and speak communism and of that sort till their pockets are empty.

BUTLER: Is money worthier than man?

SPIKES: Then what? Money is a marvelous mirror which can reflect ugly things beautiful and trivial, grand. A joke from a wealthy mouth would make many people laugh, even though they hear it for the eleventh time.

BUTLER: Is that girl a gold digger?

SPIKES: *(looking at WOODY and to BUTLER)* Something like that.

Enter SPADE closing the door behind him.

Ah! Here comes SPADE

BUTLER: *(to SPADE)* What did he say? Why did he send for you?

SPADE: We are going to lose our chance.

WOODY: Why SPADE?

SPADE: *(to BUTLER)* Have you told this matter to anyone before us?

BUTLER: No, not even to my shadow..!

SPADE: They all know about that, the doctor, the teacher and the priest. They made a plot exactly like us. He asked me to help them and...

WOODY: *(interrupting)* When are they going to dig him out?

SPADE: At the same time while we dig.

WOODY: *(hopelessly)* Everything is lost at last.

BUTLER: WOODY, be confident. Don't give up your dreams and ambitions! We can make it.

SPADE: I have an idea in my mind.

ALL THE OTHERS TOGETHER: Tell it then.

SPADE: I think it will not work.

Everyone walks across the room, pretending thinking.

SPADE: I have an idea.

SPIKES: Does it work?

SPADE: Listen to me carefully. Tomorrow at night, I will be there along with other three near MR.RICH's grave. While I'm digging the grave, you, people in disguise come to the spot. Make them unconscious by slamming them behind.

WOODY: Will it not cause any peril?

SPIKES: *(to WOODY)* Don't you know the survival of the fittest evolution theory?

SPADE: Come back! Come back! I will also fall pretending unconscious after digging out the corpse. You take the corpse anywhere and return it to the pit after taking out the stones.

SPIKES: I have a doubt. Is it one or many stones?

BUTLER: I think many.

SPIKES: How many?

SPADE: Come back! Come back! Okay, I think there will be no arguments against this matter within you further.

WOODY: You are a greater thinker, SPADE.

SPIKES: Man's brain works more efficiently, if there is any instant pay for its strain.

WOODY: Then why your mind doesn't work ever?

SPIKES: I have a problem with my mind. It never works under compulsion.

ᖘᖘᖘ

11
Scene 10

Morning, in the following day. In the drawing room of DR.SAWBONES's house. REV.BENEDICT is sitting in a chair and DR.SAWBONES is tilting a colourless solution in a glass jar.

REV.BENEDICT: What are you doing?

DR.SAWBONES: *(loudly)* This is a beverage I've invented especially for the sleepless people who are suffering from insomnia. It'll give instant sleep if someone drinks even a drop. I'm going to obtain patent for this with the name 'Somnasol' after all our expeditions are over.

REV.BENEDICT: We, ourselves may need this after. I'm already sleepless. *(Silence)* Is the fellow trustworthy?

DR.SAWBONES: *(loudly)* Which fellow?

REV.BENEDICT: That cousin of MARK. What is the need for him now? We've our own gravedigger with us.

DR.SAWBONES: *(loudly)* Does SPADE know how to sell those stones and all other underground formalities to get a...

REV.BENEDICT: *(interrupting)* We'll be five in number then.

DR.SAWBONES: *(loudly)* RAIDER was already told everything and he is on the way. We can't get rid of him anymore.

REV.BENEDICT: Then, we are five to share. Does it worth that much?

DR.SAWBONES: *(loudly)* What do you mean? Do you want to give an equal share to SPADE too? A worker is a worker. We can pay him double the amount what he gets for a dig. It could be more than enough for him.

REV.BENEDICT: What can we do if he demands for more?

DR.SAWBONES: *(loudly)* Pch..! You don't know about these people. There are plenty of ways and things to tackle the poor ones. There are two traditions to make them submissive. One is under threat and the other is by love. There are possibilities to protest against you if they are suppressed under threat but never can raise voice against you if they are shown even an ounce of love. Love is a cunning way of authority over one's freedom. A handful of rice soaked with sympathy is worthier than their rights for them if they are given that at a right time. They are ready to lick even your legs if you know how to pat them on their heads. *(Pause.)* Be calm.

Knocks at the door. DR.SAWBONES places the jar on the table and opens the door. Enter MARK, preceding RAIDER and ROOKY.

MARK: *(in a hurry)* He is RAIDER and he is ROOKY.

Both DR.SAWBONES and REV.BENEDICT smile awkwardly to them and questioningly look at MARK.

ROOKY is RAIDER's apprentice. He is very helpful.

REV.BENEDICT: *(murmuring)* We'll be six in number then.

DR.SAWBONES: gestures MARK to follow him. They enter into another room leaving the three behind. REV.BENEDICT is so nervous in the presence of the two strangers before him. To avoid eye contact and conversation with them, he turns towards the door in which DR.SAWBONES and MARK went in.

RAIDER: *(to REV.BENEDICT)* Hello sir, excuse me. Hello, sir? Hello, sir? *(REV.BENEDICT does not hear him)* What the man deaf or something?

RAIDER looks around the room and fetches the jar from the table and drinks the solution for water. ROOKY also drinks and both yawn continuously. They become unable to speak, do some stunts to get attention from REV.BENEDICT who is unaware of everything. At last, they faint. DR.SAWBONES and MARK come in, seeing them unconscious.

DR.SAWBONES: *(loudly and desperately to REV.BENEDICT)* What happen to them?

REV.BENEDICT: *(looking at fainted RAIDER and ROOKY)* I don't know?

DR.SAWBONES: *(looking the half emptied jar)* What did you do then?

REV.BENEDICT: I did nothing.

MARK goes near them and splashes the solution from the jar on their faces while DR.SAWBONES and REV.BENEDICT are conversing. Then he also tries to drink it.

DR.SAWBONES: *(looking at MARK)* Oh! You stop!

But MARK has taken few sips and drops the jar on the floor. It breaks.

(angrily) You worthless fool! You have spoilt everything. My Somnasol!

MARK starts yawning.

REV.BENEDICT: *(to DR.SAWBONES)* Calm yourself! Be patient! Be patient! *(to MARK)* What you and your people have done is utter nonsense. It is not water. It is a tonic to make one sleep. One should get permission before he is yet to use other's things or else this sort of things will happen.

MARK: *(yawns)* I'm extremely sorry *(yawns)* I don't know... *(yawns)*

DR.SAWBONES: You stop your bloody pardons. What are you going to do with this people now? It is already time to go to the graveyard. They cannot wakeup for two or more days if my experiment really works.

MARK: Do you have any anti-sleep solution? *(yawns)*

DR.SAWBONES: *(angrily)* I have pesticide to kill you all the foolish pigs.

REV.BENEDICT: Leave them here. We have SPADE. We four can make it.

DR.SAWBONES: *(to MARK)* I'm not going to give anything to your useless fellows. You have to pay for this my wasted energy. Come let's go.

MARK: *(yawns)* What do we do with these *(yawns)* fellows?

DR.SAWBONES: Let us lock the door outside and go. I think they cannot open their eyes at least for fifty two and half hours. Come, let's move.

MARK: *(yawns)* Let us pray and go.

REV.BENEDICT: *(happily)* I was yet to say.

DR.SAWBONES: Come! Come! We have no time to sing psalms or dance.

REV.BENEDICT: *(praying)* Oh god! I'm holding devils tail with the trust in you. Please help me.

They go out leaving RAIDER and ROOKY.

ppp

12
Scene 11

Under a street lamp at night, stand WOODY, SPIKES and BUTLER.

BUTLER: Shall we go now?

WOODY: No, they should have to take it out. It will take time.

BUTLER: Do you remember a thing?

WOODY: What is it?

BUTLER: SPADE told us to come in disguise. We forgot it.

SPIKES: Yes, what can we do now?

WOODY: I have a kerchief to hide my face. Look there! Two men are coming.

SPIKES: Who are they? I've never seen them before. *(There come RAIDER and ROOKY)* They are coming towards us.

RAIDER: Hello! *(yawns)* excuse me, where is the graveyard here? *(yawns)* *(ROOKY is also yawning continuously)*

BUTLER: Who are you?

RAIDER: We are archaeologists.

BUTLER: What! What are you going to do there?

RAIDER: It's none of your business. Show the way to *(yawns)* graveyard.

BOTH WOODY AND SPIKES: *(showing their hands opposite to each other)* This way!

ROOKY: Are you *(yawns)* playing? Do you know with whom you are *(yawns)* speaking? *(Pointing to RAIDER:)* He has all the right and authority to arrest you funny people. *(yawns)*

BUTLER: Pardon us, sir. They are drunkards. I will show the right way, come behind me.

RAIDER: No, you no need to come. Show us the way.

BUTLER: *(shows the direction, SPIKES has shown before)* This way!

Both yet to leave and RAIDER turns

RAIDER: You should not tell about us to anyone and *(yawns)* should not try to trace us, *(yawns)* understand!

They leave.

BUTLER: *(in a hurry)* What can we do now? Someone has sent for the police.

SPIKES: I don't think they are police. They may fakes.

BUTLER: What are you saying?

SPIKES: Do you believe them? Does the police department recruit these bugs and worms?

WOODY: They may be of some different branch of the department. They told something the name..! I forgot.

BUTLER: Darkeopolice!

WOODY: Yeah! That's it. We have to rescue our people. We have to rush to the graveyard.

SPIKES: Let them be caught.

WOODY: SPADE is also there. He will show us also.

BUTLER: Let them dig. We have shown them only the wrong direction now. They will never reach the graveyard today.

WOODY: Don't speak nonsense BUTLER. They are police. They sniff better than us.

BUTLER: Move, then. Let's not waste even a quarter of a second now.

They go.

ppp

13

Scene 12

---•♡•---

Meanwhile, in the graveyard, REV.BENEDICT, DR.SAWBONES, MARK and SPADE are standing around a grave. SPADE, wrapped him up with a blanket, has his tools, the crowbar, spade, etc. with him.

DR.SAWBONES: *(to SPADE)* When are they going to build the tombstone here?

SPADE: May be tomorrow!

MARK: I feel too dizzy. *(yawns)* Can I have a nap here? *(yawns)*

REV.BENEDICT: What fellow you are to ask this? Do you come here to sleep?

DR.SAWBONES: *(to SPADE, pointing MARK)* Bury him too along with MR.RICH, a bad for anything fellow.

SPADE starts to dig with his crowbar and DR.SAWBONES with the spade starts to help him.

REV.BENEDICT: Oh virgin mother! Save us from the curse of your son.

DR.SAWBONES: He's started howling.

MARK: *(yawns)* I can't stand anymore! *(He faints)*

REV.BENEDICT: Hey..! Hey..! Look here!

Both DR.SAWBONES and SPADE stop their work and rushed towards the fallen teacher.

DR.SAWBONES: *(checking him)* He is sleepy. That's all! We can continue.

REV.BENEDICT: Look. He's shivering like a wet cat. Give your cloth SPADE. We need to wrap him up.

Both REV.BENEDICT and SPADE completely wraps MARK with the blanket and places him a few feet apart from the grave.

DR.SAWBONES: *(loudly to REV.BENEDICT)* You want a share to simply stand and stare at us. Dig this grave or go to the gate to watch for any trespassers.

REV.BENEDICT turns to go.

SPADE: No, no, he should be here.

WOODY (Voice over): *(mimicking a harsh voice)* Police! Police!

Both DR.SAWBONES and SPADE get trembled.

SPADE: *(shouting)* Who are you?

WOODY (Voice over): *(mimicking a harsh voice)* Someone has informed the police. They are on the way here to arrest you.

REV.BENEDICT: *(trembling)* What! What shall we do now?

DR.SAWBONES: Police has traced us.

REV.BENEDICT: Police..? *(He starts running)*

SPADE: Hey, stop!

While he turns towards the direction where REV.BENEDICT is running, the crowbar, he holds, hits DR.SAWBONES's left eye.

DR.SAWBONES: Ah! My eye..! *(crying aloud)* Ooh! Blood!

He too starts running in the direction, REV.BENEDICT has gone. Following him is SPADE. All the three has gone leaving the sleeping teacher behind. The graveyard is silent for a while. A few minutes later, enter both RAIDER and ROOKY.

RAIDER: Ah..! *(yawns)* Finally, we have made it.

ROOKY: *(fearfully looking at the blanket wrapped teacher)* Look..! Something is there.

RAIDER: That might be the *(yawns)* corpse.

ROOKY: Where are the others?

RAIDER: Look there! Something box like.

ROOKY: *(takes the box and opens)* This contains scissors, knives, holder, cotton...

RAIDER: *(interrupting him)* Stop! Not even a minute to spare. Take that box and follow me.

He takes MARK on his shoulder and they exit.

▷▷▷

14

Scene 13

———⸺♡⸺———

In DR.SAWBONES's house, MARK is lying in a bed, bare bodied. His stomach is dressed with bandages. Both DR.SAWBONES and REV.BENEDICT are sitting in chairs beside the bed. The right eye of DR.SAWBONES is bandaged and the right hand of REV.BENEDICT is in shoulder sling, bandaged and he is counting the rosaries with that hand.

REV.BENEDICT: Brushing teeth with a broomstick is a bloody thing to do. God has saved us from it.

DR.SAWBONES: The major lose is for me. I have lost an eye, my surgical box, a window of my house and my everlasting invention.

MARK: And also your intention!

DR.SAWBONES: Don't bash your senseless sermons, please, MARK. You're the root cause for everything happened. I hate you speak..!

Enter SPADE

SPADE: May I come in? Oh! What happens to you all?

DR.SAWBONES: Where have you been so for? We have not seen you since that night.

SPADE: I was accompanying them to build the tomb over MR.RICH's grave. *(Looking at REV.BENEDICT, loudly)* How did you break your hand father?

REV.BENEDICT: Oh! That day, I fell into a puddle *(sighs)* I called you SPADE but you didn't mind me and vanished in the dark.

SPADE: *(loudly)* Sorry father, I did not hear you.

REV.BENEDICT: I don't think so.

SPADE: *(pointing to MARK)* What happened to him?

DR.SAWBONES: His cousin practised surgery in his abdomen in that night. They took him mistakenly for MR.RICH's corpse.

SPADE: Did they cut open his stomach?

DR.SAWBONES: Yeah! Damaged a kidney too!

SPADE: Is he alright now?

DR.SAWBONES: It'll take time to recover well completely.

MARK: *(Sobbing)* I understood a thing thoroughly now. Anyone can but never should a teacher.

DR.SAWBONES: I've a doubt SPADE. Who alarmed that night?

SPADE: How do I know, sir? I was also with you, then.

DR.SAWBONES: We did a big mistake by making that two fellows involve in our plot.

MARK: Sometimes mistakes make things better.

SPADE: I agree sir. Errors are only to...

DR.SAWBONES: *(interrupting)* Okay! Stop! Don't try to justify your wrongs and errors, as every loser do. A loss is a loss and never should be justified.

SPADE: Well, sir! *(loudly to REV.BENEDICT)* Are you coming now with me father? Everyone is searching for you. I've told them that you've a typical viral fever.

DR.SAWBONES: I've a doubt SPADE. Where were your friends, those carpenters, that night?

SPADE: *(to REV.BENEDICT not minding to DR.SAWBONES)* Come, father! Let's move.

They Exit.

DR.SAWBONES: I think everyone knows everything but the modified fact is everyone is innocent.

MARK: What do you think about me sir?

DR.SAWBONES: *(sarcastically)* Take rest my friend. You shouldn't talk. That'll endanger your life and mine too.

▷▷▷

15
Scene 14

Exactly the same environment as in the first scene. An empty room except for a stool in a corner. On it where an empty old candelabrum. On the wall above, hangs a rosary with a cross. Voices hear outside.

VOICE OF SPIKES: I think he's not returned, WOODY.

VOICE OF WOODY: Look but the door is unlocked.

VOICE OF SPIKES: Let's get in, then.

Enter both WOODY and SPIKES

SPIKES: No one and nothing is here.

WOODY: *(looking at the corner)* Look there! Our stool! *(He goes and takes it)* The candelabrum?

SPIKES: Take it also.

WOODY: Here is a rosary.

SPIKES: Take it also.

WOODY: Look here SPIKES.

SPIKES: Where?

WOODY: Here! *(Pointing to the floor)* This small part is surfaced newly with concrete. May be some looted things inside. I've heard nothing good about the fellow of this house.

SPIKES: *(goes and stamps his leg on the portion)* Yes, I hear a different sound. You're right. Place all these things right there. We'll come at night.

WOODY: Does it work? I'm afraid that it'll also...

SPIKES: *(interrupting)* Don't be a pessimist. Fortune aids only the optimists. Come, let's move and make preparations.

WOODY: Do we have to inform SPADE and BUTLER too..?

SPIKES: No, we two can do.

They Exit.

CURTAIN

ppp

www.ingramcontent.com/pod-product-compliance
Lightning Source LLC
LaVergne TN
LVHW042001060526
838200LV00041B/1826